MY FIRST JOURNEY

JP Viaggiatore

My First Journey

www.jpviaggiatore.com/english.html

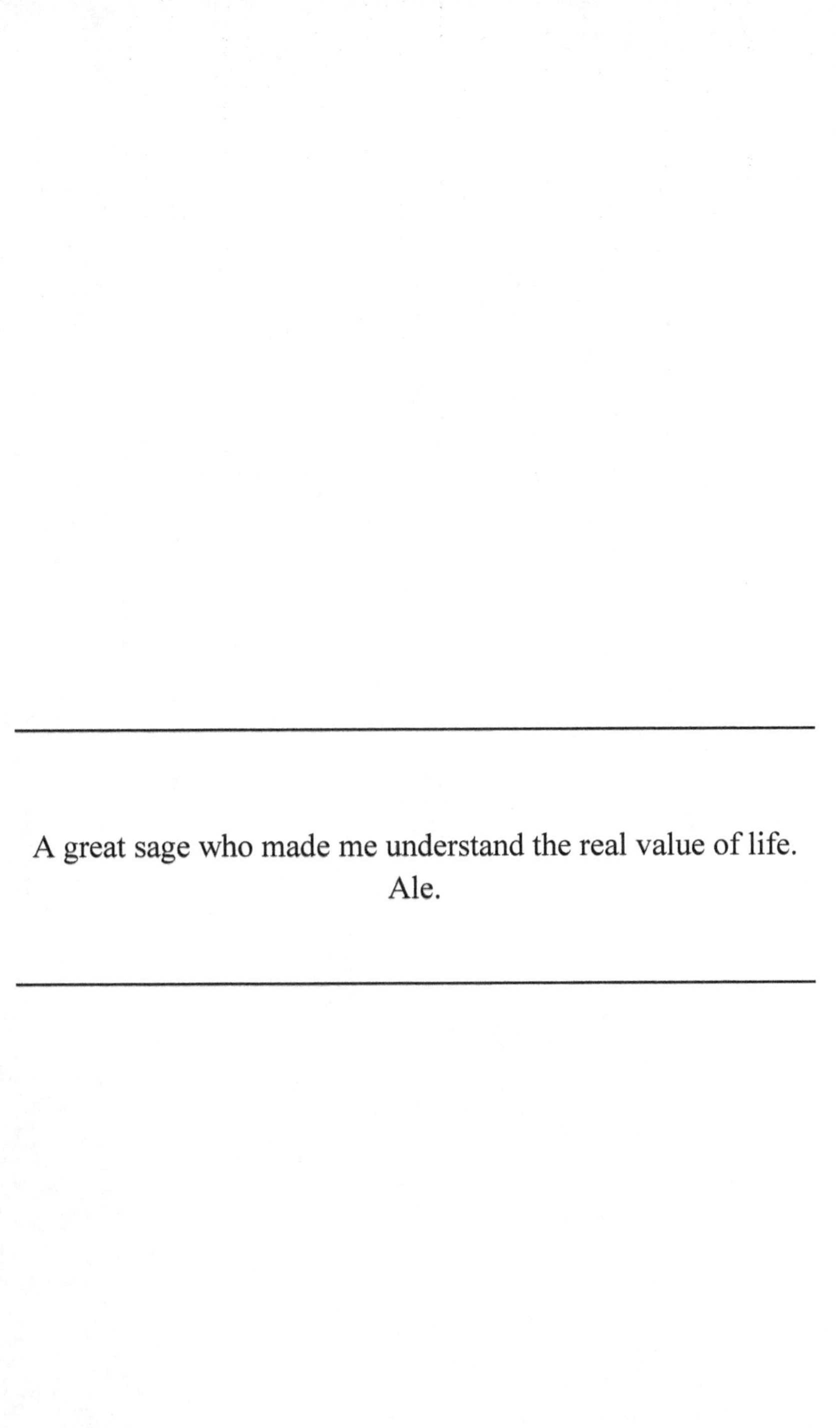

A great sage who made me understand the real value of life.
Ale.

Prologue

Some time ago, I understood that all my life experiences leave me with innumerable and valuable lessons. Today, after having the opportunity to read this book, I can reaffirm that no experiences are any more significant than others; there are simply experiences that will help us to grow and to understand the world to which we belong, in a more humane, more conscientious, and more sensitive way.

I have long been convinced that there is no such thing as a casual occurrence. A purpose exists for each circumstance that confronts us; for this reason, life itself often becomes a great personal challenge; one in which winners are not rewarded, nor losers commiserated. What is important and real, is learning to live as adventurers; those who leave behind all fears, accusations, solitude, and uncertainty. This is the essence that the author convincingly manages to portray in these pages.

This is a very captivating story. The author adeptly transforms his readers into the various characters, depending on the spiritual stage of life in which we find ourselves. Consequently, the way in which we can travel through his prose is marvelous, an authentic itinerary through the most visceral emotions and magical sensations.

This book is the story of many of us, showing us that we have the tools to discover more intensely the splendor of life and the clarity to live fully with the guidance and sense of happiness.

We all endure moments of deep hopelessness and internal conflicts; however, life can, in unexpected ways and sometimes without even noticing it, force us to climb to the top of the mountain to confront our inner selves, and teach us that if we are only willing to understand and value our existence and everything around us, is it possible to heal ourselves, all while maintaining our humility, strength and above all, love.

Carolina Gonzalez

While admiring nature on a March day at the top of a mountain, I felt a warm, gentle breeze carrying my worries away—worries that even I failed to understand, brought on by the complex thoughts racing through my brain. I let myself be carried away in admiration of that the little squirrels that ran and jumped from tree to tree, and made me feel as if time was at a standstill, and that this moment was the only thing that existed.

A subtle smile appeared on my face, despite the sadness that my heart held. Without wanting to disguise it, and leaving all the prejudices aside, trying to be free, I did not hold back my tears.

I was tired of fighting; I was exhausted from following a path paved by jagged rocks. I did not know what options to take, what to say, or what to think. Dejected, depressed, and unhappy, and with tears in my eyes of desperation to keep fighting and not getting anywhere, I thought to end this pain; this suffering. I did not feel like living anymore; nothing made sense; nothing* would make me change my mind. Just then, however, I heard a faint sound that made me turn around, and I saw something that would change my life forever.

I was astonished when I saw three very tall beings standing next to me. Their appearance was a bit strange: they resembled humans, had a Caucasian complexion, white hair, and wore white outfits with very fine golden belts. They all looked very kind.

Although I was impressed seeing these 'giants,' I did not feel afraid in the least. Their presence was calming. I did not imagine that at that moment, a different world full of possibilities would open up for me.

For some reason, I listened with my mind what they wanted to tell me. I never thought that telepathic communication really existed, but there it was. I was communicating with them, understanding everything they were telling me, and to my surprise, was able to respond.

I understood that what I always thought I had known about telepathy was far from reality. I had always believed that telepathy consisted of thinking in words what one wanted to communicate, and repeating it in the mind. I soon realized that telepathic communication is nothing like that at all. It is a type of immediate communication without needing to think about what is meant to say; instead, simply communicating what one wants to inform, without repeating in the mind with words. We just communicate, we exchange information, and we can do all this, without even knowing how it was done; that is to say, this is a process of simply exchanging information, and not using literal words.

In the midst of the fascination with all that I was living, two of those beings extended their arms, inviting me to follow them.

"Who are you and where are you taking me?" I asked.

With much tenderness and sympathy, one of them answered me, "Don't worry, follow us and you will understand."

I felt protected; I had never felt anything like this in my life, much less about beings I barely knew.

The four of us started descending the mountain. I locked myself in my thoughts that made me be aware of everything that could happen, with all the serenity and peace that infected me.

"Very soon you will see and you will experience things that you never could have imagined", one of them replied.

Something thought-provoking, abstract, in my thoughts and for some reason full of joy, I understood that everything in my life was going to change. Although I didn't know anything about what was to come, I soon understood that those beings were not from this world and that my mission was just beginning.

Arriving at the base of the mountain, I noticed some branches out of place covering an entrance; with subtlety, one of the beings removed the branches to clear the area, while the other two beings led me through a narrow entrance, where I noticed something extraordinary.

My eyes could not believe what they were seeing at that moment: It was a giant spaceship! Metal-colored; similar to the flying saucers that many people who have had encounters of the third kind manage to draw. However, the front of this "ship" was oval, and the back was slightly elongated. It was suspended from the floor and it managed to camouflage perfectly with nature.

"Now you understand who we are?" One of them asked me.

"I think so" ... I answered timidly.

"We come from another planet. Our mission is to find people like you when they are ready. All this is to help them grow spiritually and prepare them to save the world."

"Save the world?" I asked.

"Yes, this planet is populated with people, beings like you; each one arrives, learns, and in one way or another assists humanity. Some are contacted, and others are simply born with the need to help, and according to the experiences they have, they learn what they need to know in order to fulfill the mission for which they were born."

"So, I was born with that mission?" I asked.

"Have you not wondered what you were born to do, but you feel the need to help humanity?"

"Yes, many times I ask myself that question; even just a moment ago I was thinking about that. I think that's the reason why I came to this mountain; to try to find answers."

"That is right, and that is the reason that we are here."

One of them raised his right hand pointing towards the "ship," and to my amazement, a door opened and a large ramp extended to its right. The two beings to either side of me invited me to enter, and for some reason, without a moment's hesitation, I followed them, went up, entered, and the door closed behind me.

"This 'ship' is the vehicle we use to move from dimension to dimension", one of them replied.

"Dimension to dimension? I don't understand."

"We come from another planet. In our world, each one of us is assigned to find beings from different planets, and dimensional planes to prepare, help, and teach. Our mission is to train you, so that your experience makes the people of your planet aware, and raise their consciousness towards a common good."

"But why did you choose me?"

"Because you're ready. And actually, you were the one who called us."

"I called you?"

With a compassionate smile one of them answered, "That is right."

"And how did I call you? I had never seen you before in my life!"

"A few times when you had doubts, other times when you asked yourself why you came to this world, or whenever you questioned the reason for being, it caused a portal to generate in our dimensional plane, which we call a "Portal of request;" in other words, on our planet we are assigned to find beings, depending on the portal of request."

"Portal of request?" I asked.

"Imagine a newborn child. When the baby cries, a need is created, either because the baby is hungry, maybe the baby wants attention, or maybe the baby is in pain. Then, the mother turns to the child, upon hearing the baby cry; this stimulus is the portal of request. Now, the difference is that in our world, not every being generates a portal of request. For example, if someone on this planet has some moment of doubt, and needs answers, many times these uncertainties are appeased by the angels assigned to each person on this planet."

"Do angels really exist?" I asked.

"Angels are as real as you or us." he assured me.

"So, why don't they help us?"

Always with a very nice smile, and full of emotion, he answered: "They are protecting you all the time, but there is a rule—they only interfere on two occasions: when you ask for protection, or when it is not yet time to leave this world."

"Leave this world?"

"That's right. You call it 'dying'" but 'death' does not exist, the experience of this plane simply ends, allowing you to live a new experience."

"But ... God! I have so many questions."

"It's ok, you'll see that everything will be answered. Now, let me ask you something: if you had the opportunity to travel through time to the past, what time would you choose?"

I was mentally silent for a few seconds. I tried to visualize myself and I wanted to respond appropriately. Different times were going through my mind, but there was one that prominently stood out, so I answered – "even if I were not a believer, I would love to go to the beginning of humanity."

"That's it. This 'ship' as you call it, is a vehicle that travels from dimension to dimension as I explained, and time is part of the dimensional planes."

Shocked at what I had heard, for a moment I felt that my body was paralyzed; I did not know if all this was real, because in my thoughts I questioned many things. On the one hand, knowing these beings was something unreal, and now he told me that they also traveled in time. *But how was it possible?* I thought.

One of the beings with much tenderness in his eyes, and with the same warm and simple smile, took my shoulders with both hands, and in a gentle, mental tone, he told me: "All exists, everything is possible. Traveling in time, is simply an altered dimensional trip, depending on the point of departure of the traveler; that is, when a being physically travels in time, one is actually traveling to a parallel universe in accordance with the universal laws."

"Parallel universe? So, it's not really traveling through time, but rather to another dimension?"

"You said it—traveling in time is merely a trip to another present. Similarly, there is a way to travel to the future without going to another parallel universe, by using speed-space. The difference in this case is that the traveler would disappear and would not be able to return, unless they use another parallel universe. But they would never return to the universe from which started, but rather to an alternate parallel universe."

"I'm still in doubt, because if I travel through time, how would I know if I'm in another parallel universe and not the universe from which I started?" I inquired.

"Because there are always some differences from the original universe; for example, if you travel to the past and would like to return to your present, when you return you may notice some changes; therefore, you might see some construction that does not exist in the original universe, or perhaps some color that you know would not exist in this new universe you reach. Everything depends on the changes you have made in the past, and these will affect the present you are traveling to. It is here where universal laws come into play: if you make a change, you have to pay for it and you will be affected according to the changes you have made in the parallel universe. That is one of the reasons that no one can ever return to the original universe, because traveling itself manifests change, even if it is minimal and passes unnoticed."

"I understand. But now I have another doubt. If I travel to the past and stay some time there, when I return, will I see myself a little older than the rest of the people I know?"

"No, on the contrary, you would look a little younger than the others."

"Younger? I don't understand."

"Yes, first let me clarify an issue: if, for example, you travel to the past and stay there for a year, when you return to your present, the missing time would be compensated for, and you would not come back to the moment you left, but a year later, and the reason that you would look a little younger than the others is that when you travel, you always undergo a process of purification. With this process, the cells of your body are regenerated, and as a result, a slow-aging effect is produced."

"And why is the time that I am absent, compensated for?" I asked.

"To avoid precisely that: aging faster than others."

"At some point, when one travels in time, could you find your…self?"

"Yes, there are times when someone travels to a parallel universe occupied by one's self, but this does not happen very often since one would always go to a different parallel universe, and it is forbidden to travel to one's own past. Although I can assure you that you will be visited by yourself three times, and likewise you will visit an alternate self once in your life."

"How am I going to visit myself, if you just told me that I cannot travel to my own past?"

"Let me explain; you cannot visit your own past before traveling, but once you go to the past for the first time, a portal is opened that makes a referential point to which you can go."

Again, the mental silence, as a telepathic pause echoed in my mind. This information was new to me. I had so many doubts that I could keep churning about in my thoughts all day, but my eagerness to travel became evident.

"When can I travel to the past?" I asked.

"First, we must take you to our planet. You have to learn many things before you will have the requisite knowledge, wisdom, and experience. When you have learned what you must learn, you are free to travel in time; however, you will have to take into account some things; once you travel, there is no turning back—you will never be the same again. You will live many experiences, you will obtain wisdom and knowledge, you will understand many things that you do not understand today, and you will have on your shoulders the weight of responsibility to remind you that your mission is to help humanity ascend to a spiritual level and in turn, save many lives."

A fear spread throughout my body. I had not noticed the magnitude of what all this entailed; Suddenly, I realized that I had not considered my family, either. It was one thing to imagine seeing them again, and quite another to actually do it. *Was I ready? Would not it be better to say goodbye to everyone before traveling? What if I don't see them again?* I thought.

One of them looked at me with affection, as if seeing a loved one. "Don't worry, you will see them again. You are ready, I assure you," he replied.

I tried to leave my fears behind; I tried to put in check all my emotions. I breathed deeply, summoned my courage, and let myself be carried away by the trust that those beings emanated, so I answered.

"Okay, but ... how and when will I come back?"

"Do not worry; all the instructions will be given to you once you are prepared, and purified. As I already told you; we are going to travel to our planet. Our tour will last one day, so we'll bring you back tomorrow."

Having said this, those beings directed me toward a room with a very white light. The space was very extensive, almost completely empty except for a metal box throughout the center. It had no windows, but it had two doors: the main entrance through which I entered, and another back door that connected to another room.

"Here is where the purification process takes place. This same process is also done when traveling through time, with the minor difference that when you travel through time, you cannot bring with you any matter—no tangible material at all," one of them replied.

"How long does this process last?" I asked.

"The moment you tell us that you are ready to travel to our planet, we will offer you a drink, which will act in your body as a pre-cleaning agent, and will begin the purification process. Once purified, we will be ready to begin the dimensional journey to our planet."

"Okay, I think I'm ready," I said.

"Remember that we are travelers, and we assure you; you are more ready than you think," one of them replied.

"So, when do we start?" I asked anxiously.

In a kind of telepathic chorus, the three beings responded simultaneously: "Right now."

At that moment, one of the beings took out of his pocket a small glass bottle containing a translucent liquid, immediately approached me and commented:

"Drink this liquid; it will prepare your body for the pre-cleaning."

Without thinking twice, I took the jar, opened it and enjoyed its sweet, refreshing taste. I felt that my body had more energy than I could imagine, I felt relaxed and at the same time full of life. I felt almost impervious to harm, and that I was ready for everything that came. I was confident, and an inner joy radiated throughout my whole being.

"How do you feel?" one of them asked.

"Spectacular! I have never felt this way in my life," I replied.

"Well, now it's time for us to leave the room for the purification to begin."

"I'm ready!" I responded with great enthusiasm.

The three beings left the room, the door suddenly closed, and I was left in my mental silence. I already knew what was going to happen, and as if the time were synchronized, I began to hear a little buzzing inside my ears. At that moment, I understood that my purification process had begun.

A few minutes passed before that buzzing in my ears ceased, and the door opened. I began to walk as if I somehow possessed innate instructions on what to do. Even though my body and my mind were connected, it was almost impossible to have absolute awareness of my impulses.

When I was done, I walked into the other room. Without knowing how, I noticed that the three beings were

waiting for me. I also saw that this room was very similar to the purification room, but was smaller and somewhat oval.

"You are purified. Now we can travel," one of them replied.

"I'm a bit anxious, not really knowing what awaits me, and that gives me doubts," I said.

"Don't worry. Doubt makes us cautious and is* a form of self-preservation; this is normal, but very soon you will see many new things and you will learn with each one of them."

"Okay, I have a lot of emotion and uncertainty at the same time. I already want to leave, but first, if possible, I would like to know your names." I insisted.

"We do not have names because we recognize ourselves by our energetic essence. But we understand your need to name everything. If you wish, you can call me 'Number One.' Pointing to his other companions, he said, "You can call him 'Number Two,' and him 'Number Three'."

"I understand," I said appreciatively, looking at them and attempting a slight bow.

The three beings looked at me with their tender eyes, and did the same, understanding the meaning of my gratitude.

Suddenly 'One' said: "It's time to travel."

'Two' and 'Three' nodded, sat down on two very tall metal chairs, and began to move some kind of controls that were in the cabin.

Almost immediately, I could feel a very slight vibration that the ship made. I understood that I was traveling to their planet and could feel my anxiety increase.

I fell into a kind of trance. I was in awe of colors that I had never seen in my life. I observed figures and forms intertwined with each other. For me; those few seconds traveling were more real than all my years lived. It seemed as if my whole life had been a dream and that I was finally awake.

Again, the doubts and concerns came to my head. I didn't know what to expect or how to react. My thoughts were occupied with questions and I felt a little lonely. Despite being amazed by this experience, fear entered my heart and I wished to go back. Inside my mind, a torrent of thoughts raced through me: *What if something happens to me there? What if I don't see my family again? What if I can't return? What if...?*

Suddenly the ship stopped vibrating, and 'One' with great joy and enthusiasm, exclaimed:

"We have arrived!"

"Now you are going to know a new planet; you will find new things for yourself and you will learn a lot. Try to take everything calmly and with acceptance, because there are going to be things that you never imagined even existed," 'One' replied.

'Two' and 'Three' got up from their chairs, and going up to the door, touched the edges, causing the door to open, forming the same ramp by which we had gone up.

From inside the ship, it seemed as if it was a very sunny day with no clouds in the sky, but once I crossed the exit door, guided by 'One', I noticed that there was no sun and that the sky was completely white.

"Where is the sun?" I asked very curiously.

"I want you to know that on our planet there is no sun. Our atmosphere consists of tiny energy particles that prevent heat from emanating, and that is why the climate is mild. Also, because our planet is very similar in size to yours, the force of gravity is very similar."

"So, it never gets dark?" I asked.

"Never," 'One' answered. "Now follow us."

Very slowly we began to descend the ramp, while I perceived that the ship was suspended from the ground, and that the only thing that was touching it was the ramp door that had just opened.

I felt a handful of emotions when my right foot touched the ground for the first time. I was bewildered; happy but nervous. Uncertainty with waves of doubt ran through my head. *How did I travel? How did I get here?* I tried to understand everything that was happening to me, but it was impossible. I could only let myself live the moment, and continue being guided by those beings.

While we walked along a path of smooth, yellow stones, I observed the nature surrounding us. I could not believe how such beauty was possible. On my right side, there were some kind of fluorescent purple plants, while on my left side, I saw a large, crystal-clear spring. An immense lake reflected the white of the sky. It was impossible to comprehend how it could radiate so many different colors; it was like a diamond shining in the sun.

I could also smell a fresh scent of nature: it was something similar to the smell of rain falling on the earth. I could feel that freshness of a place free of contamination. It seemed as if the plants created the purest oxygen I'd ever breathed, that no place on my planet could match.

Suddenly, 'One', with great enthusiasm, and with total admiration told me, "Look at all of this, observe these plants, look at those animals; everything is so simple, but at the same time so perfect. We live in our respective worlds and many times we forget to admire this beauty. You all worry about your problems and lock yourselves in a cube with no way out. The worries do not allow us to evolve; they keep our minds occupied, and that keeps us from being free. If you all only understood everything we are, everything we have, and everything we can do, you all would be so happy," 'One' continued. "You come from another world; there are many different things there, but simple things like these, are still there. Do not let yourself be contaminated; keep enjoying these simple things, and always love unconditionally."

This time I was more amazed with everything he had told me; even if I knew that 'One' could read my thoughts, it did not cease to amaze me. It was not easy to take on everything I was experiencing, let alone comprehend everything I was learning.

The air, full of that pure oxygen, provided complete relaxation, and although I didn't know where I was going, I did not care; the feeling of confidence and security trapped my worries in the depths of my ego.

The minutes became so long that they seemed eternal, and while the three beings communicated with each other, I kept hiding behind my mental silence.

Suddenly we came to a very open place that surprised me. My whole body was paralyzed. My heart stirred, and my gaze, as if in a trance, was focused on that enormous edifice, because I had never seen anything like it; it was a giant, golden pyramid.

"This pyramid is one of many, where we all gather to acquire energy; it is a means of feeding. Another one, because we consume vegetables and we drink water same as you. Come in, and let us show you," 'One' stated.

Without further ado, I followed them without fear, allowing myself to be led by* all the possibilities of change that life was pleasantly bestowing upon me.

I admired the great monument, and as I approached, I marveled at how wonderful it shone in the middle of this big space full of nature; with spectacular colors accompanied by the flight of 'birds' very similar to those I already knew.

I also heard a kind of a song produced by people, which surprised me. It was the first time I heard voices! They were deep voices like that of adult men. *So, they can talk too?* I thought.

"We also have a language; however, this form of communication is not used often, since we tend to communicate all telepathically. When we utter sounds of protection, we use our physical voices."

"I don't understand," I replied.

"Look, the voices that you hear are songs generated by inhabitants of this planet. They are our companions who are producing sounds of protection. The vibrations of these songs cause a type of protection and are generated in the place where the song is made. It is not necessary to protect oneself in that way, since there are innumerable more advanced forms of protection without the need to use the voice, but this protection song is an old custom of ours."

Once having arrived at the entrance of this great pyramid, I saw how two beings whom I assumed to be guards, standing at the entrance. They greeted the three beings in the form of an embrace, while they bowed to me. Then, telepathically, one of them said, "Welcome."

This gesture made me question some things, because neither of them seemed surprised, as if they were accustomed to bringing humans to their planet.

"Come on, come with us!" 'One' said happily.

Letting myself be carried away by my curiosity, I followed them again, because I wanted to know what was inside this great pyramid; I also wanted to be able to see the owners of the voices I had heard.

Inside, I noticed a very large space. Then in the middle, there was a round, blue energy almost touching the ground that illuminated the entire pyramid inside with a white ray of light that came from the top of the pyramid. I could also count eighteen giant elders around this energy, who were holding hands, forming a perfect circle and singing a kind of mantra.

"What is that energy ball?" I asked curiously.

"That energy is the means of feeding. We absorb what our body needs in the moment. It's something like a recharge," 'One' answered.

"But didn't you tell me that you also eat vegetables and drink water?"

"Of course, we have a physical body. To maintain it, we have not lost the habit of consuming something physical. However, little by little, we are reaching a state where we are only going to consume energy," 'One' continued. "It is something similar to the change that people experience when they stop consuming meat, because no matter how much they want to leave it, the body asks for it until they get used to not needing it."

"You don't consume meat?"

"No, our ancestors put a stop to that practice long ago; our bodies cannot resist those kinds of dead cells, because if we did, our bodies would get sick."

"Then is it bad to eat meat?" I asked.

"It is not a question of 'right' or 'wrong.' When you elevate your consciousness, you change your way of living; you realize many things that your body craves, and you act according to what you need. When you acquire this knowledge, you understand that the consumption of meat generates diseases of all kinds; In addition, the organism does not digest the meat completely, while with vegetables, they are used to the maximum, and the waste, the body cleanses it on its own. But you have to keep in mind that everything is a process; If you are used to consuming meat, you have to detox little by little, because any drastic change can generate an alteration in your body, and that causes problems for you, generally."

'One', taking me by the hand and leaving 'Two' and 'Three' where they were, said, "Come with me, I want you to meet someone."

Without argument, I let myself be guided as I always did; I felt like a child letting go of this wise giant.

We crossed where the energy was, and the beings singing. I could also see that inside this great pyramid there was some kind of a huge living room with a giant, circular, glass door. Inside the living room I could see a man in a blue outfit and golden belt, sitting on a golden chair as well, appearing to be waiting for someone.

It was not long before 'One' opened the door and they both greeted each other with a hug. It seemed as if they were great friends who were greeting each other after not seeing each other for a long time.

'One', ignoring what I was thinking, and leaving me alone with that man, smiled at me and left the room, closing the glass door that muted all external sound.

"Relax and sit down," the blue-eyed, white-haired man suggested, pointing at a slightly smaller chair.

Without thinking much and with butterflies in my stomach, I sat down.

"Do you know why you're here?" The man asked me.

Looking uncertain, but guided by the confidence that this man exuded, I answered, "To learn?"

"More than that, we all learn from everyone, but your greatest mission is: to share your experiences and teach them to whomever wants to receive them.

"Teach? But..."

"This communication, even if you do not believe it, comes from within you."

"From inside? But there are so many things that I don't understand," I answered.

"Telepathy is an exchange of information. I can explain many things to you—for example, what I am saying at this moment—but you interpret the information according to your knowledge, and even more than that, to your wisdom. That is why different languages are not necessary, because in the spiritual world, each one receives according to their level."

"Then I could not communicate with a person of a lower level?" I asked.

"Spiritual beings do not have higher or lower levels than others; they are only at different frequencies. Each being lives his or her life according to the experiences they have had, because how could you expect someone who has never been taught values, to act correctly? It would be very unfair to judge them, don't you think?"

"Well, yes, but... What if they do something wrong? Should they not be judged?" I asked.

"What is bad for you?" The man asked me, observing my expressions carefully.

"To rob, for example."

"Have you ever stolen?"

"Never!" I proudly answered him.

"Did you ever remain silent after someone gave you back too much change after a purchase?"

"Yes, but that's not stealing."

"What is stealing for you?" He asked me.

"Well, to take something that does not belong to you."

"Exactly," the man replied.

At that moment I felt like a fool; I just realized that I had stolen. I felt dirty, I did not feel worthy to communicate with such a wise man.

Suddenly, the man interrupted me with a gentle, friendly smile. "Do not worry; nothing in this life is bad; everything depends on how we look at it, and how we feel about it. There are many people who steal out of necessity. Maybe they do not do it with bad intentions, or maybe they really need it, but for one reason or another, they have to do it. Also, they may have some impediment to work. Some may never have been taught values, or perhaps experiences in life made them that way, but that does not make them bad people. They are simply living how they have to live, and their spiritual level is not high or low, it is simply a spiritual level according to the experiences if which they must live. Remember that nothing is by chance*. Everything happens for a reason, and whatever you do, you are going to pay for it. If you do something 'bad', and you feel guilty, you are going to carry a weight, but if you do not feel guilty, then you will be free."

"So, if I do something that, in my opinion, is bad, but I do not feel guilty, I don't have to pay for it?"

"If you know you're doing something wrong, but you do not feel guilty, why would you pay for that? Would it not seem unfair?"

"Yes, but...what about innocent people who are imprisoned? Why do they often have to pay?"

"Physical laws work very different from spiritual laws. If not, how do you explain that judges, or leaders, order a killer to be sentenced to death? Wouldn't that make them murderers, too? I tell you that earthly laws need to be amended, because they are made by men and no one is free from sin."

"How can you acquire knowledge or the wisdom necessary to create physical laws that are really effectual?" I asked.

"Simply by remembering that pride nourishes knowledge, and humility nourishes wisdom!" The man answered.

There was an avalanche of ideas that only increased my admiration for this being, who seemed to have an answer for everything, but I still had many questions.

"Is it bad to kill?"

"As I said, nothing in this world is 'bad,' *per se*; everything depends on the intention with which the acts are committed. I'll give you an example: if you kill someone by accident. Why would you have to pay for it if it was not your intention to kill? Maybe with earthly rules you would pay, but spiritually, you will be free, as long as you do not let yourself be influenced by guilt."

"So, if it is done deliberately, is it bad?"

"Have you ever killed?" The man asked.

"Never!" I replied.

"You haven't ever killed an animal?"

"I've killed insects, but it's different."

"What makes it different? I'm telling you that killing is killing—period. It is the taking of a life."

"Yes, but..."

"What makes you be better than an animal?"

"The fact that we have consciousness," I replied hastily.

"Then, don't you think that because we are aware we should act differently? If we are aware of our actions, then why kill? Would it not then make us guiltier than those who have no consciousness?"

My mental silence, like a deep echo, was pointing out the feeling of guilt that grew with each beat of my heart. Each time, I felt smaller next to this great being; I did not know what to do or how to react; I wanted to open a hole in the ground to deposit all my shame.

The man with his benevolent look and with his ever-present tranquility, looked me in the eye and with a soft, mental tone, said:

"There is nothing to worry about. As I told you, nothing is bad; all our acts are experiences that should be lived. From this, we learn to become better beings, and at the same time, raise awareness through wisdom. When we reach a high state of consciousness, we realize that it does not make sense to hurt anyone; that we should always act with love, and that we should always give the best of ourselves to all beings." The man continued. "Beings that do not yet raise their consciousness, act according to what they need to learn. Many times, the simple circumstances of life have not let them be what they really are. Many of the people in your world who commit crimes continue to learn, and the feeling of guilt does not allow them to be free. The moment they learn to forgive themselves, they can advance!"

"And the people who kill, but do not feel any remorse. What's wrong with them?" I asked.

"There are people with mental illness; sometimes as a result of some trauma and in other cases, it is simply born within them. There are also people who are deceived into committing crimes, but some do not feel guilt since they do it pursuing an ideal. In these cases they don't have to pay for it in a spiritual matter, since their conscience is free of guilt, but they do create what one might call a 'Karmatic chain,' and in this case, the one cannot get rid of it, until one becomes aware of what one did, and forgives oneself."

"And what exactly is the Karmatic chain?"

"It is something that only works spiritually; that is, it is a kind of universal record that is recorded in the universe. For example: if you do something to someone, a spiritual record is universally created; if what you do is wrong, and you forgive yourself from the heart, it is erased in a sense, but if you do not forgive yourself, or are not aware of what you did, that record is still latent until you free yourself by paying for it. Many times, you pay it yourself in life, and many other times you pay with your offspring, but all this is so that you become aware of your behavior, and free yourself from it by forgiving yourself, and thus raising your consciousness. Remember, sometimes we call the 'bad' things 'bad,' by our own ignorance, but if we observe, we realize that everything* is for learning—to raise our level of consciousness."

"What do I need to know to raise my consciousness?"

"You need to get rid of three things: fear, guilt, and anger; these three feelings take the most energy. Fear is an obstacle that prevents you from moving forward. Guilt keeps your heart from being free. And anger takes away your inner peace."

"How do I not feel fear, guilt, or anger?"

"We feel fear when there is no knowledge of something; someone who ignores something will feel fear of the unknown. When we really understand something, fear disappears completely. On the other hand, the feeling of guilt is expressed, when we understand that we have done something wrong; therefore, it is necessary to always act in the best way. And finally, anger results from a lack of wisdom; we lose control of our emotions and allow them to govern us. For this reason, it is necessary to learn, if we're to behave wisely!"

A little confused, I asked, "What is the difference between knowledge and wisdom?"

"Knowledge is to understand why. Wisdom is knowing how to act."

"Have you ever felt fear, guilt, or anger?" I asked.

Peacefully, yet enthusiastically, it seemed, that man answered me: "Of course! While we have a physical body, all these emotions will accompany us; for this reason, it is necessary to obtain wisdom, to understand things and always act correctly. It is normal for a being to fail because we are all in a constant state of learning, we all make mistakes. The important thing is to learn from them, thereby acquiring wisdom; that is why it is very important to take away our sins, since they are that which condemn our own consciousness. When we forgive others, we are also forgiving ourselves, as this frees us from our own guilt of feelings of anger or resentment toward someone and cleanses our soul."

"How can I forgive someone who has hurt me so much?"

"Realizing that when someone hurts another, it is out of ignorance; that person acts according to what he or she knows, according to values, or to the things they have learned in life. Many times, they are not aware of their actions, or other times they ignore the consequences."

"But it's so hard to forgive," I replied.

"It is difficult when you keep clinging to the pain caused by others, but the damage you are doing, is only to yourself. You keep the wound open and do not let it heal. That causes trauma and takes away the essence of your own being because you always act defensively, protecting your open wound, and if another person touches it without you wanting to, it will continue to hurt. That is why it is essential that you forgive others, as well as yourself, realize that we all learn, and always love one another."

At that moment, almost immediately, the man approached me, hugged me and I could not help but cry as I had never cried before.

"You are a great being; don't forget it," the man concluded.

Although my tears continued to run down my cheeks, I felt inner peace. I could visualize all the people who at some point in my life had hurt me, and with all my heart, I forgave them as well as myself.

The man extended his right arm, and, inviting me to stand, with sweetness in his eyes, told me: "Well done; now you are free!"

Oriented by intuition, 'One' entered the room, understanding the freedom I felt in my heart, and knew that I was ready.

"Come on, it's time for you to receive an infusion of energy," 'One' replied.

Then, saying goodbye to the 'man' with a thank-you bow and wiping my tears away, I started to follow my friend.

We left the room and began to walk toward the source of energy that was in the center of the pyramid.

When we were approaching, I noticed that the elders stopped singing, then formed a line where everyone began to put their hands on the energy to absorb it, and it, in turn, glowed white on the palms of their hands.

"Let's touch it," 'One' suggested.

'One' approached the source of energy as if he were already used to handling it, and put his hands on it. Immediately, I could see a glow on his palms when it made contact with him. 'One', turning his head and directing his gaze toward me, telepathically told me: "Come, caress the energy."

My curious spirit and eagerness to know everything, gave my legs permission to walk toward the energy source.

When I felt the blue energy, there was a tingling in my hands. 'One' looked at me, and I could feel him communicating; "Do not limit yourself, absorb the energy."

Looking at him with uncertainty, I answered: "But... how do I do it?"

"You have to believe in yourself. Imagine, visualize, and appreciate how your body absorbs energy," 'One' replied.

Closing my eyes and concentrating on 'One''s instructions, I began to imagine that my body absorbed a little energy. And to my surprise, at that very moment, I could feel the energy entering through every pore of my skin through my slightly unctuous hands; and experiencing thus, a very pleasant heat ran through my entire body, from my hands to the tips of my feet. I felt alive, with an abundance of energy; I radiated peace, I felt admiration for those beings. I felt new. I just felt indescribably happy.

'One', realizing that I had already absorbed the necessary energy, and that I was ready and renewed, took my hand and told me: "Now we are going to another place that I want to show you."

Filled with emotion, I let myself go like a very small child. I could observe how we were leaving the pyramid while the group of elders was absorbing energy from the source. 'Two' and 'Three' came after us. It seemed as if they knew exactly how to behave and as if they were used to this kind of interaction with humans.

While we were leaving the pyramid, many doubts were nagging at me. I did not know whether to ask 'One', or if it was better to remain quiet and wait for him to teach me.

"You want to ask me something?" 'One' asked.

"I still have many questions. I would like to know so many things; for example, what are angels like? Is it true that they have wings?"

Without hesitation, 'One', knowing the images I had been conjuring in my mind, sweetly answered; "Everyone sees angels according to their spiritual eyes. Angels do not have a tangible form—they are beings of light, but when they represent people, they do so according to what people feel comfortable with."

"And is it true that they are always protecting us?" I asked.

"Whenever we ask, they protect us. They are made available to us; to take care of us, to guide us, and to protect us. There is something that is important to know: they do not know what it is to feel cold, or to feel hungry. Since they do not have a physical body, this is, to them, a foreign concept. That is why they always love us unconditionally. There are also other types of beings that do not know that we exist, but this I'll explain to you when we meet again," 'One' answered.

More and more doubts came to my mind. I had always been very curious, and wanted to know everything. I remember when I was little, every night when I saw the stars, I asked my mother things about space, or things about existence; for example, I questioned a lot about what happened after death, or if it was true that spirits existed, but I never got answers. Well, even if my mother had a lot of knowledge, she could not know everything. That made me kind of frustrated, and invited me to inquire about myself, but I realized that I still did not find answers. And now I had the opportunity to ask about the things I had

always wanted to know. So without thinking, I asked, "What happens* after we die?"

"As you already know, death' does not exist. It is simply a process of change that we all go through. Each person is purified according to their needs, and in the process, it is determined whether it is necessary to be born again or if they can continue to the next step."

"To be born again?" I asked.

"When you're ready, I'll explain it to you in more depth."

I struggled with my curiosity because I wanted to know many things, but I finally understood the reasoning, and I held on to what 'One' wished me to know.

'One', understanding everything that went through my head, replied, "There is always time for everything. When we see each other for the second time, your conscience will understand and know many more things."

As we arrived at the main door, I felt relaxed yet imbued with energy. I felt like a new being, but there was something that surprised me a lot; I was so focused on what I was asking 'One' that I didn't see how 'Two' and 'Three' had come so quickly to the exit where they were waiting for us. It was at that moment when I realized that the roles had changed; now 'Two' and 'Three' were guiding us while 'One' was teaching me.

Once out of the pyramid, it was impossible not to linger to admire such beauty. It was a golden pyramid reflecting the sky and the beautiful colors that nature shared—a scene I'd never forget. Also, in the distance, one could see the 'birds' and the different 'animals' with many similarities to those that inhabit my planet.

While 'One' and I let ourselves be guided by 'Two' and 'Three', I walked while I was immersed in my thoughts of admiration and curiosity. I could see how we were heading down another road, also formed by yellow stones that went into the 'forest.' I saw colors in nature that I had never before perceived; I tried to analyze them, but I simply could not, so I had no choice but to admire them and enjoy this great landscape.

"Do you like everything you see?" 'One' asked.

"Very much." I replied cheerfully.

"When we see something new, we admire it, because our curiosity and our experience compels us to know and explore, but once we get used to it, we leave this feeling of admiration aside and we forget the beauty we have in front of our eyes. That's why it's very important to keep that flame of admiration alive for everything, so we always enjoy the moment, and that helps us to be happy." 'One' continued. "It's like when you meet a special person in your life. At first, there is admiration, and that also makes you special to them, but when you begin to fall victim to monotony, you get used to special acts being part of the routine, and little by little, that flame goes out. That is why it is very important to keep it lit with the humble acts you can have for someone, and always enjoy the moments, to be able to love."

Having heard this, a doubt had crept into my head; I had not seen any women on this planet, so I asked, "Are there women on this planet?"

"Of course, we have partners, just as you do. At this moment we are heading there, so that you also get to know them," 'One' answered.

We came to a path where there were very familiar trees almost like the ones on earth, the main difference being that they were purple, and extremely tall, but many of them also bore fruit. On the other hand, I could also see an entrance made with 'branches' in the form of an arch, creating a kind of path that went into the 'forest.' 'Two' and 'Three' looked very excited when crossing the branches, while 'One' looked me in the eyes and encouraged me to continue.

"Come, we're nearly there," 'One' said.

Without thinking much, I decided to let myself be guided by 'One' and follow 'Two' and 'Three', our guides.

After a few minutes, we came into a clearing, and I could see in the distance a kind of village in the open countryside, where several beings—dressed in the same way as my beloved traveling companions—could be seen.

"We have arrived."

Looking around me, I asked, "What is this place?"

"This place is where we live; here are our families. Look closely at this place; see how we spend time here."

As we approached, we could see 'Men,' 'Women' and 'Children;' I could not believe it, everything was so similar to my planet that if it were not for their imposing stature, it might have gone unnoticed. The women were almost as tall as 'One', 'Two', and 'Three', while some children were of my size and others a little bigger.

I noticed how some beings from this village greeted in the form of an embrace to 'One', 'Two' and 'Three', and they would do the same. Afterwards, I saw how each one of them made me sympathetically welcome, that I answered with reciprocity in the form of a greeting.

There were children playing, some were running and others were doing something that caught my attention: each was running toward the 'trees,' and with the palms of their hands they took turns touching the trunks, then squealed with delight.

'One', with a fixed gaze, saw that I did not understand anything that was happening; With a gesture of tenderness, he said: "Do you see those children playing?"

"Yes, but what are they doing?" I asked.

"Their game entails leaving telepathic messages in the trees, for the others to decipher. It is very common on this planet." 'One' answered. "People on your planet also play this game."

Surprised, I asked, "Really?"

"That's right; there are many people who practice things that we have taught them. There are many things that you do not know yet, but you will get to know them when the moment is right."

All this had fallen on me like a bucket of cold water. There were so many things that I did not know, that with every moment, I was feeling increasingly ignorant.

"Is there anything else I can learn?" I asked.

"Do you want to ask me something in particular?" 'One' asked.

"Well, I don't know, I have so many questions; for example: Is there such a thing as 'magic'?"

"Yes, there are several levels of magic; there are the tricks that illusionists perform in shows, but they are just that—tricks to entertain people. But there is another type of magic that is real. You call it 'black magic' and 'white magic,' but they are the same."

"I've heard of them. They are the same?"

"That's right; this kind of magic on your planet uses physical things to accomplish a goal. This type of magic creates certain karmic chain depending on one's intention. There are people on your planet who practice this kind of magic to hurt someone or to protect someone, but I will also explain this to you when you see me again," 'One' continued. "There is also another type of spiritual magic. These are powers that can be acquired by any being, depending on the state of purity at the spiritual level, because that is when the famous mental powers can be achieved."

"What…? So mental powers really exist?"

"Even now we are practicing one of them—telepathy."

Excited, I asked. "Is there any other mental power that you can show me?"

'One' pointed to some small rocks and asked me, "Do you see that black stone?"

"Yes," I answered.

'One' looked intently at the stone, causing it to tremble slightly at first, and then more vigorously until it sprang up and traveled through the air into 'One''s extended palm.

I could not believe what I was seeing. I had heard of telekinesis, but I had always believed it to be a myth.

'One', as always, knowing what was going through my head, replied, "There are many people on your planet who are capable of this."

"Seriously?" I asked skeptically. "Then why have I never heard about them?"

"When someone acquires mental powers, it is as a result of, not only their wisdom, but their spiritual purity."

"Spiritual purity?"

"That's right. To achieve this kind of thing, it is necessary to cleanse our spirit, and not let pride rule us or inflate our ego. This prevents the natural flow of purpose, and the channels become obstructed. This is why you have not seen anyone who does it publicly; when someone does it to praise themselves or purely out of entertainment, the power becomes isolated. Let's say that someone who can really do it, is fully aware of their talent, and have no need to prove it."

With the head tilted a little to one side, I asked him, "Could I do it?"

"When you see me again, I will teach you how." 'One' answered.

Impatient to learn, I turned my gaze to 'One' and asked, "Why are there so many things that I cannot know at this time?"

"Although you have learned many things, you still have much more to learn. Even though at this moment your spirit is clean, it is necessary that you put into practice everything you have learned. Everything is a process of personal growth and liberation. That's why, when we meet again, you will understand why you were not ready. Remember that the pleasure of life is more attainable when a real understanding can be avoided!"

A 'child' came running up to me, and he pulled my hand to go play. A little doubtful and somewhat regretfully, I looked at 'One', asking him with his eyes to rescue me from this situation, but 'One', with a knowing smile, and a little wink, said, "Don't worry, go and play, be free; nobody here judges you; this game is also part of your learning."

I understood that it was time to let myself be carried away by my instinct, and that I needed to rid myself of concern for* what others might say. So, leaving my prejudices behind, I followed my new little friend—even though he was taller than I—with white hair, and green eyes.

I noticed how the children all knew that I was not part of this planet, and with unexpected kindness, each one of them tried to explain the game to me.

I was able to receive the plethora of telepathic information coming from all the children with no problem. It is impossible to explain how I could receive and understand all this information without having to process it. I understood that the purpose of the game was to try to leave telepathic messages in a tree, then go to the rest of the trees and collect the information left by the other players, as well as ascertain who had left each message, and then to meet again in the middle of the field. The first to get to the center of the field with all the messages collected, knowing exactly who left each message, wins the game.

It seemed easy enough, since apparently I was masterfully managing telepathy; then without further ado, once everything was explained, all the children in a mental chorus said, "The game starts now."

I quickly ran to the first tree I saw. I approached it, placing the palms of my hands on its trunk, trying to leave my message. Suddenly, I froze; I did not know how to leave my message, and even if I did, what kind of message would I leave?

Nervous, I looked around to see what the children did, and I tried to do the same. I put my hands back on the tree, closed my eyes, and visualized a message from the depths of my heart, toward the living essence of the tree: "I am very grateful to learn so much."

When I opened my eyes, I could see how the children ran to different trees, deciphering the messages, then went to the next tree and left more messages. So, without wasting any time, and wishing to win, I did the same.

I came to a small tree where I had seen one of the children leave a message. Timidly, I put my hands on the tree to receive its message; but to my great disappointment, I could not receive anything, in spite the intensity of my thoughts. It was very difficult for me to believe how it was possible to communicate with all of the children so easily, but receiving a simple message from a tree was, for me, impossible.

A bit discouraged, I ran to the next closest tree to do the same. *Maybe nobody had left messages on that tree*, I thought. But to my surprise, and ending any semblance of hope I might have had, I obtained the same result. No message was captured by my mind. Then, already resigned, I went to the center of the field to wait for the children who had not yet finished.

Sad and bored, I saw how, one by one, they were arriving at the center of the field where I was waiting for them. Everyone sat on the blue-green lawn in a mental silence to wait for the rest of the group. It was there that I understood that one of the rules of the game was that nobody could communicate with anyone until the last had arrived.

When the last being arrived, everyone looked at me with the expectation that I would tell them my messages. Very distressed, I looked at them to make them understand that I had not been able to receive any. One of the 'girls' with a look of pity said, "Don't despair. You are new to this. You will soon understand and will succeed."

Suddenly, the one who had arrived behind me began to look at all the children to decipher each of their messages; Suddenly, to my surprise, he glanced my way, saying something that restored my spirits, to some degree: "I am very grateful to learn so much."

My skin bristled, my heart stirred, and I could not help but feel a surge of emotion, because I had not been able to receive messages, but at least I had managed to leave mine on the tree, and that made me giddy with happiness.

Once the game was over, my grateful companions said goodbye, with tender hugs. Sadly, I embraced them too, because in such a short time I had become very fond of them.

I began to walk toward 'One', and I could not help but feel two things: on the one hand, pride, and on the other, disappointment. Still lingering in my mind was the shame for not being able to receive the messages expressed in the trees. *Should I have used any special technique? Is it not possible for humans to do it?* After much analysis, I realized that I had no answer. According to what 'One' had told me, on my planet there were people who practiced this game. This made the second question moot.

As I approached 'One', he stared at my brown eyes, and asked me, "What's wrong? Why are you sad?"

"As you already know, I wasn't able to receive the messages from the trees, but... why?"

"Don't distress; look, I'll explain. When you communicate with us, it is possible because we facilitate the process. We accommodate you as a courtesy. Remember, we have a lifetime of practice. We can adjust to the spiritual level of each being. But this is all very new to you. The moment a person starts talking, telepathy becomes secondary. It is for this reason that you were not able to receive the messages left in the trees. At that moment, it was you alone, and you lack the requisite practice in telepathy."

"At the moment we start talking, it is….secondary? I don't understand."

"That's right, babies bring with them the open spiritual essence. This essence closes as they adjust to the physical world; that is why, when they begin to use words as a form of communication, telepathy is left behind until it is completely forgotten. Also, when they close their spiritual eyes, they stop seeing spiritual beings, since in their new world they only need their physical eyes. It is for this reason that, on your planet, children are more adept at seeing angels and spiritual beings; unfortunately, they get desensitized as they mature, and then they have to re-sensitize to wake up again."

"What do you mean by desensitized?"

"The adults of your planet often desensitize their young without meaning to; that is to say, they do not allow children to be free; they teach them beliefs and ideas that they think are good, and they change their own spiritual instincts. In other words, when a child sees things or talks to a spiritual being, adults convince them that it is merely their imagination, and end up closing off their spiritual essence. They make this mistake often, and when children grow up, they end up doing the same thing their negligent parents did, creating an endless cycle," 'One' continued. "I can tell you that there are many on your planet who still feel this spiritual essence, and have a desire to help. The important thing is to follow that instinct and not let the flame be extinguished."

Beckoning me to follow him, 'One' said, "Let's go over there. I want you to share with us. It's time to eat."

Getting ready to acquire knowledge, and without wanting to bother him by asking him more questions, I started to follow him. I realized that we were heading to a very large, round 'house' made of a metal similar to aluminum and covered with glass.

"How are these constructed—with aluminum?" I asked.

"No, this metal does not exist on your planet; it is very malleable and depending on the process used, it can become thinner than aluminum, and at the same time, stronger than iron."

"The ships that you use—are they also made with this material?"

"That's right. This metal is nearly impervious. That's why it is so commonly used. We need to travel to different dimensional planes. In addition, we also use something very similar to the electric waves that you all use, and this metal is much better conductor of electricity than silver. Due to the diffusion process we use with gold, it makes it more resistant to oxidation."

"So, you also use gold and silver?"

"Of course. The pyramid you saw is made of gold. On this planet are many metals that you use on your planet, and also others that you all do not know."

"And what's the name of the metal you told me about?" I asked.

"As you already know, we do not label things, because we know everything by its essence. This communication is telepathic, and I communicate everything according to the energetic essence of each thing. In this way, you interpret everything according to your knowledge, and although you are learning new things, your subconscious is responsible for associating the things you already know with the new things you see, to create a new thought. But within yourself, you have more information than you think you have."

"So I know more things than I think I know?" I asked.

"All beings, including the people of your planet, are born with intuitive information, and depending on the spiritual plane where you are born, you adapt, using the information necessary to start your new life; the information that you don't use is set aside, but there it is, waiting to be awakened."

"And, what information do I not use?"

"Before you knew me, you did not use telepathy, for example. If you were born on our planet, you would let this information flow, and it would seem very normal for you."

As my head was swimming, I thought of a question, and because my curiosity was greater than my grief, I asked, "Why was I born on the planet Earth and not on another planet?—on this planet, for example."

"You were born with a mission. Your goal is to teach the people of your planet how to have a better world."

"And how do I do this?" I asked.

"You will find the way. The important thing is that you do not let go of your spiritual flame. Anyway, this is not your only journey; it's just your first." Excitedly, 'One' continued. "We will see you many times and we will continue guiding your way."

"This is all so confusing... I really do not feel worthy to have such a huge mission and with such responsibility," I continued. "In addition, I'm not perfect, I make so many mistakes!"

"And who has not made mistakes? The important thing is to know how to handle them and keep growing. Take cheer, my friend! You will see how things fit in their place. We know that you are the right person. Someday you will understand what I am saying to you." 'One' continued with a bit of nostalgia. "When you return to your world, you will go through many tests. You are going to want to reveal everything that you have experienced here, and also you will want to teach people everything you have learned, but there will be people who will not have the ears to listen, and this will frustrate you; however, it is necessary that you undergo these circumstances, so that you become stronger. You have to know that you will be bringing them knowledge that is difficult to convey. Imagine a person who was born blind; for them, that world full of darkness would be normal, and no matter how much you describe to them the things that you see, they cannot really know what they are like, without acquiring sight. And once they do, they will place greater value on this new world full of colors and shapes, than a person who is used to 'seeing' their whole life. It is for this reason that a person must go through a moment of doubt, because when they awaken, they realize the true value of life!"

A few moments later, 'Two' and 'Three' interrupted us to let us know that the food was ready. 'One', pointing at the entrance of the house, invited me to enter. Somewhat shyly, I followed 'Two' and 'Three', while 'One' took up the rear.

I observed many things similar to those I already knew: there were chairs and tables made of glass and various metals. The floor and walls were white, made of stone, were smooth and shiny. I could tell they had recently been polished.

While walking down the corridor, I could see very large rooms on both sides, each with an immense, rectangular, metal door, very similar to those of my planet. At the end of the corridor was another huge room without a door, which I surmised was the 'main room,' mostly because of the giant table surrounded by many chairs.

When we arrived in the 'room,' I saw a large feast set out on the table. I found it curious to see several chairs of regular size, next to the giant chairs.

"And those chairs?" I asked 'One', turning to see him.

With a* very sweet gesture, 'One' answered, "They are for you... Go sit, I will be sitting next to you."

Without asking more, I followed his request. Maybe I was boring him again with my obvious questions, and that was the last thing I wanted to do.

Sitting on one of the chairs, I noticed that to my right was a small lever. 'One', knowing my thoughts, and connecting with me telepathically, said, "That lever is for you to raise or lower the chair as needed. If you push it forward, it raises; backwards, it's lowered to the floor."

Without thinking, I began to raise the chair, but to my surprise, I saw that I was not the only one doing this; several children did the same to reach the table.

I could not contain myself, and counted the number of 'people' present. There were twenty beings, including 'men,' 'women,' 'children,' and my three friends, all together sitting at the table, ready to enjoy these succulent dishes consisting of vegetables, soups and stews; there were some strange fruit and juices, round 'muffins' next to something that looked like rice, and I also saw desserts of different sizes. I noticed how the 'men' served food to the 'children' in their little dishes; making me understand how similar humans were to these beings.

'One' did the same. He began to serve me different small portions of each dish without asking me anything.

I understood that 'One' wanted me to try everything; I wanted to give myself the opportunity to enjoy each dish, and I did so quite willingly.

I tried the rolls, since they were very similar to what I knew. I was stunned; because, even though they were a little larger than the ones I knew, and their texture was a little lighter, they tasted exactly like delicious fresh bread I knew back home, recently taken out of the oven.

"How is it possible that these rolls have the same flavor as the bread of my planet?" I asked 'One'.

"Inevitably, some places, objects and customs on your planet will seem similar to what we have here; we have extensive knowledge of different cultures," 'One' answered.

Although I could continue the conversation, and the telepathic communication would not affect anything while eating, I just wanted to concentrate on the flavors and enjoy each dish without distractions. Suspending our 'talk,' I decided to just enjoy the tastes and textures before me.

'One', understanding the situation, let me enjoy my moment; I was very excited, I was like a little boy in a candy store. There was a lot of food, and everybody (including 'One'), seemed to be enjoying every bite. I did the same and tried all the different items that were already on my plate; I ate fruits and desserts, I drank refreshing water, I took full advantage of the moment and I was able to delight myself with these delicious delicacies. Some food tasted similar to dishes I had tasted once, and there were others that did not. However, I did not want to miss this opportunity, and little by little I tasted each flavor until my stomach was satisfied, every cell of my body thanking me, and in return, invigorating and giving me an abundance of energy.

Without realizing it, we all finished eating almost at the same time; it was as if there were an invisible chronometer and each of us followed it without realizing it, or maybe, we were all connected in some inexplicable way.

'One', meanwhile, approached me, and with a tender smile said, "Let's go, it's almost time for you to return to your planet; but first, I want to show you a place."

I could not believe that this information would somehow hit reality. Maybe I was getting used to this planet, or maybe I was happy to come back. I had many

mixed emotions: I felt happiness, nostalgia, sadness, excitement, anxiety, curiosity.

"And the dishes? Who will clear the table?" I asked.

"Don't worry, someone is already in charge of that," 'One' answered.

"So, you hire someone to clean up?"

"No, nobody works on this planet," 'One' responded with an affectionate gaze.

"Then how do they do?"

"Here on our planet, we share the work depending on the tastes of each person; that is, there are those who like to cook, others like to build things, others like to care for the children, others enjoy harvesting, and so, everyone is free to do what they are passionate about."

"What if someone does not want to do anything? How do they deal with that?"

"There is no one here like that. None of us would feel good taking advantage of others. When you change your consciousness, you realize that it is rewarding to offer a service; you know that when you help others, you help yourself, for the reward of giving! it is more valuable than anything you might receive. When you give, you receive good energy, peace in your heart, purity in your conscience. When you receive something material, you only receive that one thing."

"It's time to leave," 'Two' and 'Three' replied telepathically at the same time.

I thought no more and pulled the lever back to lower the chair to the floor.

'One', 'Two', and 'Three' stood, thanking everyone at the table. They looked at each other, hugged, and cordially said their goodbyes. I also noticed how everyone who was there bowed to me and said goodbye; It was as if they knew it was my time to leave. I did the exact same thing, thanking them for everything, and for the great service I'd received. Then, my three friends gave me a well-known look and I understood with certainty that it was time to follow them again. So, walking one after the other, we exited the room, crossing the hall, until we reached the entrance.

When we left the great 'house,' 'One', with the tranquility that characterized him said, "Now we are going to a very nice place that I'm sure you'll like a lot."

'Two' and 'Three', knowing the route, began to walk on another road made of smooth stones. 'One', as always by my side explaining what I didn't understand, and I, with all the curiosity of the world, receiving the greatest knowledge imaginable, eagerly followed them down the road.

Once again, we went through many parts very similar to the ones I had already seen. There were 'trees', 'branches' and 'flowers' of different colors, there were 'animals' similar to rabbits and also 'birds' of different sizes. This whole planet was alive. The air was so pure, the 'animals' so free, the sky so white, the plants so soft. I tried in some way to look at this planet from another perspective. I wanted to discover if I could see something that I could complain about, but … everything was so utterly perfect.

My head and my eyes were overwhelmed with ecstasy. It was hard not to be able to see so much beauty. I turned my head and looked at 'Two' and 'Three'; I wanted to see if they also admired what I did, and I realized that they only focused on their path. *Maybe if they were on my planet they would act similarly,* I thought. *Then it is true what 'One' told me. We are really so used to seeing what we see every day that we do not admire what we have at the moment.*

"So it is," 'One' interrupted, knowing everything I was thinking. "None of us forget to appreciate what we have. What happens is that sometimes we focus on other things, and we overlook the beauty to allow us to better enjoy these valuable moments."

"So you do, too? Do you also forget to enjoy this nature that I am enjoying right now?" I asked.

"All of us see different things. You may see the same thing that I see and we are enjoying it in different ways; each one has lived a different life, and the value of something changes, depending on our experiences; for example, if a person from your planet, who comes from the countryside, sees a mountain, it may seem very common; since he or she is accustomed to seeing them, but a city person could enjoy it more," continued 'One'. "And, instead of a mountain, there was a building; the countryside dweller would be fascinated observing it, whereas for the person of city it would be rather mundane."

"I understand. Then 'Two' and 'Three' are not enjoying this beautiful landscape as I do, because they are used to seeing it."

"Yes, they are enjoying it, but not like you. For you, everything is new, you are seeing things you have never seen before. They on the other hand, are more focused on showing you the way to enjoy the beautiful things that this planet offers. We are enjoying watching you enjoy yourself," 'One' continued. "Look at those birds—they are enjoying this moment and they are doing it without caring what we are doing. Everyone enjoys and lives a different moment."

"Do you also enjoy traveling to my planet?" I asked.

"Of course, we admire many things that you sometimes take for granted. We have also guided many people to change the world, and you are one of them."

"I am?"

"Yes, you."

"And how am I going to change the world?"

"With love," 'One' replied.

"What is love?" I asked.

"Love is the purest feeling there is: it is a free feeling, it is something that you feel for something or for someone, without wanting to ask for anything in return."

Objectively, I answered, "I understand, it's like when a person falls in love, because he or she wants to be with that person all the time because they love them."

"Falling in love and loving are two completely different things. When you are in love with a person, you want to be with them all the time, share every moment, enjoy every opportunity, but the moment that person is missing, your soul hurts, you feel that you need them, you feel that without them you will not live. Sometimes you become stubborn, you make the mistake of becoming a controller, and you create an attachment. Conversely, when you truly love a person, you let them be free, you only want their happiness regardless of whether they are with you or not. It is a beautiful feeling, without prejudices, without attachments, without pain, because it is pure."

"Can I be in love and feel love at the same time?"

"Yes, you can be in love with a person and at the same time love them, but you have to be very careful not to obsess, because when you feel that you cannot live without them, cannot be happy without them, or without being attached to them, then you are not feeling true love."

"How do I know if I feel true love toward that person?"

"When you allow them to be free and still you are happy because they are happy."

Carried away by my doubts, I stopped to think a little. I realized that I had already gone through all the processes: I had fallen in love with someone, I had become obsessed with her, and now I know I loved her; because, although she did not want to be with me and had taken the moon that I gave her, my soul and my heart were happy to know that she was never going to be alone, because my moon would accompany her for the rest of her life.

'One', knowing the nostalgia that my heart held, looked in my eyes, and with a sensitive gaze, said, "You are a great person. You really know how to love!"

'Two' and 'Three', very excited, recited in telepathic tone the same phrase that always made me happy. "We have arrived!"

I looked around, trying to discover that great place they wanted so much to show me, but I saw only the same thing that I had seen the whole trip.

Was this what they wanted to show me? I thought. *We could have stayed at the beginning of the road, and I would have seen nothing different.*

"What's wrong?" 'One' asked. "Are you disappointed? How quickly did you get used to seeing all of this, that it no longer excites you?"

Obfuscated, disillusioned, and with my head down, I answered: "Well, no, but... I imagined something different."

"You were so excited enjoying the trip because you knew you were going to see something spectacular that you did not mind being happy, even for a moment, but now that you see what you see, you regret having walked," 'One' continued. "That is exactly how life is. Many times we feel excited when we have a goal or something to fight for, but when things do not go the way we want, we get depressed, and we forget how happy we were when we traveled that road that we yearned for. Life is about living and enjoying every moment, giving everything of yourself without expecting anything in return, of being constantly happy, and of loving unconditionally."

"You're right; sometimes I get carried away by emotions and forget everything I know, but I'll try to follow your advice... I'll enjoy every moment and be happy with what I have; in this case, this beautiful landscape," I replied.

'One', knowing my heart and knowing that I was still learning, did not chastise me anymore. After clearing some branches, he said, "Follow me."

Without questioning anything, I started walking behind my great friend. I followed him through a kind of short tunnel formed by branches, while my other two friends followed.

We spent a little time walking through the spacious tunnel, when I saw something spectacular: it was the same lake that I had seen before, but located at another end, due to the exit of the tunnel that faced the lake directly.

When we left the tunnel, I could see the vastness of the lake and its crystal-clear water that reflected the two beautiful, majestic mountains that protected it.

There was also something that amazed me that I still could not understand. It was that this beautiful lake produced those different colors that shone with the white reflection of the sky, something incredible.

"Why does water diffuse those different colors so bright and so beautiful?" I asked.

"Come on, let's get closer to the shore so you understand," 'One' answered.

Without disturbing him in the least, and like a happy child on a beach, I let myself be guided, while 'Two' and 'Three' were waiting for us sitting on the 'grass.'

When we approached the shore, I could let my curiosity take a rest. I could see stones inside the lake of different sizes and colors. It was a spectacular sight; it looked like a very bright rainbow radiating its most intense colors.

Then, I continued to take off my shoes, my socks, I rolled up my pants, and slowly entered the lake until the water reached my knees.

'One' stayed on the shore sitting, watching me enjoy my moment, while I jumped, ran, raised stones to admire them and then throw them back into the lake. It seemed as if nothing else existed, I did not care the judgment, nor what my friends would think, because at that moment I was free, and there was nothing to stop me.

I picked up a very small stone that had several colors. It also shone with the white reflection of the sky, and while I rotated it to observe it from all sides, it seemed to change color. I turned my gaze to 'One' and somewhat shyly, I asked, "May I keep this stone?"

'One', very calmly, and restoring my confidence, answered, "Of course, that is a gift so that whenever you see it, you will remember everything you have learned!"

"Thank you very much," I answered enthusiastically.

Wrapped in happiness, I put the small stone in the right pocket of my pants, to continue playing and jumping. It was as if time did not exist; there were no worries or prejudices; I was still enjoying my moment.

However, after a while I was a little tired, so I sat next to 'One', and the two of us each focused on the images that passed through our eyes, silently admiring that beautiful landscape.

"What do you think of all this you're seeing?" 'One' asked with his eyes lost on the horizon.

"It's something I cannot describe. It's spectacular. I never imagined anything like this in my life."

"Do you know why we brought you here?"

"No, why?" I hesitated.

"To make you realize how great God is."

As if they had thrown a bucket of cold water on me, I was paralyzed; In all the time I had been with the beings, I had not asked once about God. But taking advantage of the occasion and with no hesitancy, I inquired, "Do you know God?"

'One', with a lot of security, but at the same time with a lot of sweetness, answered, "Not only do I know God, but I am always with God.

"You can see God?"

"God is in everything and everyone. You see God when you find wonders like these and you appreciate them with all your heart, when you enjoy and appreciate what you have, when you are humble, when you forgive someone, when you love others."

"Then, God is everything?"

"God is represented in what makes you feel peace in your heart and joy in your spirit."

"Then God is not a being?"

"If we say that God is a being, we would be being selfish, because God is ubiquitous. God is in the smile of a baby, in the tenderness of an animal; God is everything and we are all part of God. This is why it is essential always to treat everyone the best way possible, since God is represented in everything and in everyone."

"I had always believed that God is a being, because since I was a child I was taught that God would punish me if I behaved badly," I replied.

"If God punishes you for your constant learning, then why would you want to learn?"

"Learning?" I asked.

"Yes, remember that the 'bad' does not exist. Making mistakes just provides more opportunities to learn; from each experience you learn to grow as a person, and if God punishes you for doing it, then what would you learn?" 'One' continued. "God does not punish; God is love, God is total understanding, God is mercy, God is union, God loves us so much, and that allows us to be free so that the reward is more rewarding when we grow spiritually."

"What about people who are born poor, or people who are born with a disease. Why does God allow that?" I asked.

"To learn and purify the soul, to be free and to grow spiritually."

"Purify the soul?"

"Yes, there are chains that must be broken, and many times they are so strong that it is necessary to experience pain in order to be able to heal; God is merciful in giving us the opportunity to feel pain, so that we know exactly what must be healed."

"Every time we suffer, we purify the soul?" I asked

"If we learn from it, yes," 'One' answered.

"Could it happen that a person suffers and never learns?"

"Of course, there are people who cling to suffering and generate more trauma that, in turn, creates more chains. That is why it is very important to learn to free yourself; learn to take away your guilt, and to understand the why of things, to act correctly."

"Well, how can a person do that?"

"You already know: by forgiving yourself and forgiving others," 'One' answered.

After saying this, my great friend 'One', pointing to that beautiful landscape that was before my eyes, asked me, "What do you see there?"

A little doubtful, I answered, "I see a beautiful lake accompanied by two great mountains."

"What else do you see?"

"I see birds flying, and the crystalline water that shines producing several colors," I answered.

"And what do you feel when you see all of this?"

I took a deep breath of pure air, and with a big smile I answered, "I feel peace, joy, tranquility."

'One' was moved. "I wanted to show you this, to explain to you that whenever you feel what you are feeling right now, remember that God is with you!"

Respectfully, 'Two' and 'Three' approached 'One' and I, sitting on the edge just in front of us in a circle.

"It's almost time to leave," 'Two' said while looking into my eyes.

Somehow, I was getting used to this new world. I loved the ambience, I liked the lifestyle, I felt great breathing this oxygen so pure. It was also true that I missed my family, but being here, my priorities began to change.

"Can I stay a little longer?" I asked.

'Two', with a tender look, grabbing my right shoulder, said, "I am sorry, it is necessary that you return; You need to complete your mission. Also, you do not have to worry; we'll see each other again."

"Eighteen hours have passed," 'Three' said encouragingly.

"Has that much time really passed?"

'One' calmly answered, "Yes, you may not feel it because your body is used to days and nights, while on this planet there is no nightfall."

"And why don't I feel tired?" I asked.

"The drink we gave you causes your cells to regenerate," 'One' answered.

"Then, you don't sleep?"

"Of course we do, but not as you do. We sleep once every three days."

"And for how long?"

"Approximately six hours."

"Six earthly hours?"

"That's right. Our communication is telepathic, and for this reason, you will always interpret time as what you already know, but time is relative, and according to the information we give you, you adapt it according to what you interpret as time. But you would be surprised if I told you that time, as you know it, does not exist!"

"Time does not exist?" I questioned.

"Remember when I told you that time is part of the dimensional planes? The way you all measure time, is to ensconce yourselves in the system. For example, If the rotation or translation of your planet were a little slower or faster, you would measure time differently. On the other hand, if you measure time according to the speed of an object, time would change. If you measure time according to the mass of an object, it would also be different. If you measure time according to the 'time' of a moment, it would also change. Therefore, only until you stop using time as a reference in your physical or mathematical equations, can you clarify things that are inexplicable to you."

"Like what?" I questioned.

"For example, there are different realities. Also, people would understand that the speed of light is not the fastest speed that exists."

"All of this is very complicated; there is so much information, that it is a little difficult to process," I said.

"Now do you understand why I always tell you everything in your 'time'? When we see each other again, I'll explain in more detail," 'One' replied, asking me with a mischievous yet tender smile.

Smiling shyly, I answered, "Now I understand."

"Let's go; it's time to return," 'One' replied, sighing, looking me in the eyes.

'Two' and 'Three' immediately stood up, understanding that it was time to leave, and started heading toward the space ship.

"Come, stand up," 'One' said, offering me his hand.

Accustomed to following the 'orders' of my great friend, I stood up without hesitation; I knew it was time to return, and no matter how much I wanted to stay, I could not.

'Two' and 'Three' went on walking along a path formed by the lawn, near the shore of the great lake. And while 'One' and I followed them, I kept observing and admiring this colorful world, full of the unexpected and illusions that always made me understand why I didn't want to leave this world, so unreal, but at the same time, so perfect.

As I went along that narrow path, I gazed upon the crystalline lake, enjoying its bright colors, emanating from the stones under the water's surface, and that, with the reflection of the white sky, made the water shine even more brilliantly.

I remembered that I had picked up one of the stones from the lake. Then putting my hand in my pocket, I took out the stone to admire it once again, it was so bright and so strange. *What a beautiful stone*, I thought. My heart was

throbbing with emotion every time I saw it... not only was it splendid with its bright colors, but it represented everything I had learned on my journey.

While I was rotating the little stone to look at it from all sides, my head tried to analyze everything that I had experienced on my trip. There were so many things that my brain grew tired trying to process so many different thoughts at the same time.

"Do not try to analyze everything. Leave that curious mind aside, and dedicate yourself to enjoy the moment now that you have it," 'One' suggested.

"I'm sorry," I said, putting my stone back in my pocket.

Smiling delicately, 'One' said, "You do not have to feel bad; take advantage of the moment and free yourself. Do not think about what has already happened, nor about what will come; just live in your present so you can make the most of it."

"You're right," I replied.

Halfway there, 'Two' and 'Three' stood still for a moment, while 'One' and I quickened our pace. When we caught up, I could hear the squeak of an animal. It was a bit strange, but I could tell it was in pain. I could see that, a short distance away, something was moving.

"Come on, follow me," 'One' said, as he walked toward the movement.

With some trepidation, I followed him, while 'Two' and 'Three' waited for us on the path.

As I got closer, I could see that it was a medium-sized animal, a little strange, but resembling a wolf: it also had four legs, its fur was a little thicker and green, its snout was flatter, and ears pointed down. It appeared to be immobilized, as it continued moaning in pain.

As we approached, I could see that its right front leg was a little crooked and hurt; and attempting to stand up, the animal kept falling down, and would then scream again.

'One' stared directly into the eyes of the animal, and magically, it stopped screaming. 'One' reached out to touch it, and immediately the animal understood that it was not in danger; On the contrary, it seemed to sense that 'One' was there to help, so it remained immobile. 'One', seeing this, put his hands on the injured leg, and I could see a purple energy emanate from my friend's hands, covering the injured area. Then, this same energy gradually turned light blue.

After a few seconds, 'One' stared at the animal again, and the animal, understanding the situation, stood on its four legs, looked at us once more, and finally ran away as if nothing had happened.

"What is this that I just witnessed?" I asked

"This animal needed help, and I helped," 'One' answered.

"But what was wrong?"

"The energy in its body did not flow properly, creating a knot. I simply untied it so that it could flow again."

"But I saw that one of the legs was hurt," I replied.

"That's right, it had broken," 'One' explained. "When we have a wound or some kind of disease, the energy of our body stops flowing freely, stagnating at some point and creating a blockage or knot. Many times, the same body, as it regenerates its cells, releases energy, until it flows correctly again. I simply accelerated this process."

"So, when a person has a disease, the same thing happens?" I asked.

"Exactly, a sick person can have any kind of virus or bacteria causing the energy not to flow properly. To treat this, he or she begins to take certain types of drugs to treat what they have, depending on the factors involved. But often, the taking of these medications, especially the chemicals (assuming they were competently prescribed and that they are really treating the disease as such), generate reactions and side effects that are very harmful to the body, also causing more energetic knots."

"And the natural medicines? They are better?"

"They are better than chemicals in terms of side effects, since they do not directly damage any part of your body, but sometimes they do not work because on your planet, there are too many viruses and bacteria that were created chemically. Another reason is that when the person is not persistent, it stops helping the body's natural immune system, making the cure a little slower," 'One' answered.

"So, what is the best way to cure someone?" I asked.

"Every time you receive spiritual wisdom, you realize that, if you learn to manage the energy, you could do many things," 'One' answered.

"Can I do it, too?"

"Of course. Any being that has a conscience can do it."

"And how do I do it?"

"For this, you have to let your energy flow properly, and it is also necessary to learn some techniques."

"What techniques do I need to learn? How do I make my energy flow properly?"

"The next time we meet, I'll show you how to do it, and how to find your own technique. For your energy to flow properly, you need to be physically and emotionally well."

"If I'm not well, does my energy not flow properly?"

"It's just as you say. If you have blockages yourself, it is very difficult to remove those of others. There are some people who do it, and some people who absorb the knots of others and keep them, but these people are not using the proper techniques, as they are slowly injuring themselves."

"Can one heal oneself?" I asked.

"Yes, you can do it yourself if you use the right technique, which then acts as a bridge to heal," 'One' answered.

"I think I'm going to understand this when you show me how, right?"

"Yes. First you need to deeply understand everything you have learned. Before you are able to multiply, you first have to know how to add."

For a moment I was pensive. My curiosity was so great that it played with my patience. Not understanding was proving difficult, especially if that would help me heal people. I anxiously wanted to have all the answers right away. But 'One' was right; I had to be patient. Maybe that was another virtue that I had to learn to control. Maybe it was a test, or maybe that was one of the requirements to gain wisdom. I did not know that yet... but, the answer was going to arrive very soon.

"It's time to move forward," 'One' said as I began to walk slowly toward my other two friends.

Without thinking much, and following 'One''s instructions, I did what I was used to doing, following my great guide, while I was adapting to the idea of my return.

Once arriving at the path formed by the lawn, 'Two' and 'Three' continued with the journey without asking anything, while 'One' and I were behind them as before.

As we walked, I was still overwhelmed by the unknown. The experience I had seen recently created doubts. Then giving freedom to my curiosity, I asked 'One', "Why did I see an energy coming out of your hands?"

'One', turning his head, and looking at me with those gray, benevolent eyes, answered, "I let you see the energy that you saw, so that you learned to discover what it represented. You saw the knot in energetic color, and as I was releasing the energy, you could see how it changed color, until the leg was completely healed. That is why it is so essential that you learn to feel the energy to perfection, since that is what you are going to use as a tool, to work when you heal someone," 'One' continued. "For this reason*, you should do everything calmly. Everything in its time, and learning from every moment, because in order to control the energy, first you have to learn to feel it. But before you can feel it, you have to know how to visualize it, and for that, you have to be in harmony with your whole being, your body, your mind, and your spirit; Therefore, you have to obtain knowledge and wisdom. In other words, you must learn how to behave correctly, using as a shield, the most important feeling of all... Love!"

An infinite feeling of happiness gave me goose bumps. I realized why I was there. At last I understood the reason for these lessons; Now I knew with certainty what 'One' had expressed to me—my mission was to help people. At last I understood that everything was a process, and that I needed to walk first, only later to fly.

'One', seeing the light that now illuminated my soul, turned his head again, and as we walked, he put his left hand on my shoulder, saying, "You have understood."

It would not be long before we arrived at a familiar place. It was the spot where I had stepped on the ground for the first time on this curious planet. Suddenly, I looked up and saw a shiny vehicle waiting for us. It was the spaceship that had brought us to this planet and the one that was going to take us back.

I had mixed feelings. I wanted to continue learning and enjoying this beautiful place, but having seen the ship again made my body and my mind feel a bit of nostalgia for my planet, and now I wanted to return.

As we approached the ship, 'Two' did the same thing that 'One' had done at the beginning of my crossing to open the ship: he raised his right arm, pointing the palm of his hand toward the ship, and the door to the ship automatically opened, waiting for us to ascend.

Without waiting long, 'Two' and 'Three' began to board the ship, while 'One', indicating the entrance, invited me in. For a moment, I was admiring this planet, and 'One', knowing that it was my moment to say goodbye, leaving the hurry aside, gave me that moment; Well, even if I knew I was going to see my friends again, I did not know if I would return to this planet.

Then seeing the sky, the plants so colorful, and observing everything around me, I said goodbye in silence. "Thank you, very nice planet, for giving me the opportunity to meet you and for having taught me so much..." Immediately, and trying to prevent my sadness from overwhelming me, I began to ascend the ramp, with my great friend accompanying me as always.

The ship closed automatically as if it knew the exact number of people who were going to enter. On the other hand, I already knew the steps to follow: first the cleaning and purification, and then the trip itself.

'One', looking straight into my eyes, and knowing as always what I was thinking, telepathically exclaimed, "This time it's going to be a little different. You will not have to undergo the purification process; you're already purified."

"Then the purification process is only done once?" I asked.

"The purification process is done as many times as necessary, but this time you do not need to do it, since our planet is purified," 'One' answered.

'Two', inviting me with a gesture, shaking his head, said, "Come with us."

Looking at 'One' in approval, and with a little sorrow, I followed him.

We went to another spacious room inside the ship where there were many buttons and command levers. I kept looking around, and I was surprised with everything I saw: there were three very large chairs. There was also something very similar to a sofa, and there were oval, metal tables. The main light was white, but the command buttons adorned it with colors. I was fascinated with everything I was observing. This ship was so big that, although I had already been in it, it was the first time I had seen this room.

At last I could see the process of piloting the ship. 'One', 'Two', and 'Three' began to move buttons that made strange sounds.

"Are you ready to travel?" 'One' asked, turning to me.

"I think so, but what do I do? Where is the seat belt?"

'One', with a kind smile, replied, "We do not need restraints. Each area of the ship is protected by anti-gravity energy that is counteracted by an inertial effect against the outside of the ship. Or do you not remember how you traveled?"

I was a little confused. There were so many details I had not realized before. Everything had happened so fast that I didn't have much time to think. Remembering how everything had been, I answered smiling, "You are right, I hadn't thought of that before. I think I was so excited to travel, I hadn't even considered it."

"Don't worry. When you get to your planet, and have time to reflect, you will remember even more things. For now, live the moment, and enjoy the experience, so that you have more things to remember."

With no need to mention it, we all knew it was time to leave, so ending the conversation, and leaning back on the big 'sofa,' I said to 'One', "I'm ready!"

Then, 'One', 'Two', and 'Three', took control of the ship, to begin the voyage home, while I just watched.

The ship began to vibrate slightly, and was then suspended, immobile and calm. In that instant, I knew that we were already traveling; I started to see colors, and also shapes. It seemed as if the speed or maybe another factor, had some effect on my senses; because apart from seeing what I saw, I felt that my body was very light, and I couldn't analyze the moment, only experience it.

After a few minutes, everything was quiet. My senses returned to normal, and my three friends stopped manipulating the controls.

"We have arrived," 'One' said as he stood up from his seat.

'Two' and 'Three' immediately left the booth to open the door. Meanwhile, 'One', staring at me, and with a bit of nostalgia that showed in his eyes, said: "It's time to leave; follow me."

Somewhat sad and disconcerted, I began to follow my great friend; I knew it was time to say goodbye, but at the same time, I was on my planet, and I wanted to set foot on the earth again.

When I got to the ramp, I noticed that 'Two' and 'Three' had already opened the door. From inside the ship, one could see the sky and the trees. Also, I could see the sun, I realized that it was a little earlier than the day before, and that it had the makings of a spectacular day.

Emotions began to surge through me; I wanted to go out, I wanted to see my family again. I wanted to climb the mountain again. I wanted to admire the beauty of my planet. I wanted to do so many things that I didn't know where to start.

'Two' and 'Three', understanding the exaltation in my heart, and knowing that it was time to say goodbye, offered me a hug. I embraced each one, knowing that I would see them again; and at the same time, I said goodbye to them, thanking them for everything: "Thank you very much for this trip, and for all the lessons," I communicated.

"Thanks to you, too; even if you do not believe it, we have learned a lot, as well," 'Two' answered.

After saying goodbye to my two great friends, 'One', heading out the exit of the ship, said, "Come with me, it's time; let's go down together."

I started to follow him, and as we descended the ramp, I noticed that we were exactly in the same place where we had left. I could see the trees, and next to them, the bushes that formed the entrance of this makeshift hiding spot. I could breathe the air of my planet, feel the soft and simple breeze. I could admire that clear blue sky, as well as listen to the sound of the animals that stoked the feeling of nostalgia.

When I stepped on the ground, my skin bristled completely. I felt immense happiness; I had returned to my planet and now I knew how much I had missed it... my eyes were filled with tears.

"I want you to know that we'll meet again when you're ready. For now, always live the moment and apply to your life all you have learned," 'One' replied.

"And when will I be ready?"

"You will be ready when you acquire wisdom; meanwhile, you are in the process of learning. You will feel sadness, anger, doubt, you will feel many things that are inevitable to experience; It's normal to feel them, you just have to learn to handle them and not let them control you. Wisdom is not in avoiding feeling the wrong things, but in knowing how to cope with them in order to act correctly! Remember that everything and everyone is part of God, and for this reason, we should always let ourselves be carried away by the feeling of love. Love everyone and everything, with all the purity and sincerity that that feeling deserves; just like that, you raise your level of consciousness."

"You're right, although I think it's not going to be easy," I answered.

"It's easier than you think," 'One' answered, continuing the communication. "Now we must go.

Remember, we will return for you, my great friend. You are a great being, we love you, and do not forget always to be happy."

With watery eyes, I embraced my great friend with all my strength. I looked like a small child hugging the leg of this giant, who with his hands calmed me, caressing my hair.

"Thanks to you for everything; I'm going to miss you a lot," I said to 'One', and while my tears ran down my cheeks, I let him go.

'One', with a soft smile, and with the tenderness that characterized his eyes, replied: "Do not give up, do not lose heart, remember that in your hands there is a great mission; do not forget it."

Turning around, my great friend went up the ramp. When he was already inside the ship, the door closed automatically. Then the ship rose slowly, until it disappeared in the blink of an eye, leaving a soft breeze in its place.

Now I was alone; I looked around, and I did not see anyone. For a moment I tried to analyze the situation, I tried to think about what had happened. I did not know what might happen next. I had no idea what to do, but, to avoid nostalgia and the feeling of loneliness, I decided to climb the mountain again.

Leaving the bushes, I started trekking toward the top, during which time I perceived that my way of seeing things had changed, because I admired everything I saw. I could feel full happiness; I was very happy to have learned so much, and was proud to be renewed.

A few minutes passed, and after walking so much, I could contemplate that spectacular view that nature gave me from the top of the mountain. So without thinking, and just letting myself capture the moment, I sat down to continue admiring so much beauty; I wanted to focus on this, I wanted to thank God for everything that was given to me. breathing the pure air, and sighing with happiness, I remembered everything I had lived.

I pondered on everything I had learned; I remembered every situation and every moment; a shower of mixed feelings began to overflow my whole being. On the one hand, I felt privileged to have learned so much, while on the other, I did not feel worthy of so much wisdom. I began to feel lonely; my friends were no longer there to calm all my doubts and give me encouragement... I felt sadness and some anxiety. I also felt fear and began to doubt everything, knowing what I had lived was so perfect; it seemed surreal. My mind began to create uncertainties that made me question whether everything had been a fantasy.

My answer would come with a big smile on my face, when I felt a small bulge in the right pocket of my pants; I reached in my hand, and removed something wonderful that shone with the reflection of the sun, generating those colors, so intense and brilliant, that it instantly relieved me of my doubts and my loneliness. It was a small, beautiful stone—a souvenir from a distant world.